Crystal the Snow Fairy

by Daisy Meadows

illustrated by Georgie Ripper

Join the Rainbow Magic Reading Challenge!

Read the story and collect your fairy points to climb the Reading Rainbow online. Turn to the back of the book for details!

This book is worth 5 points.

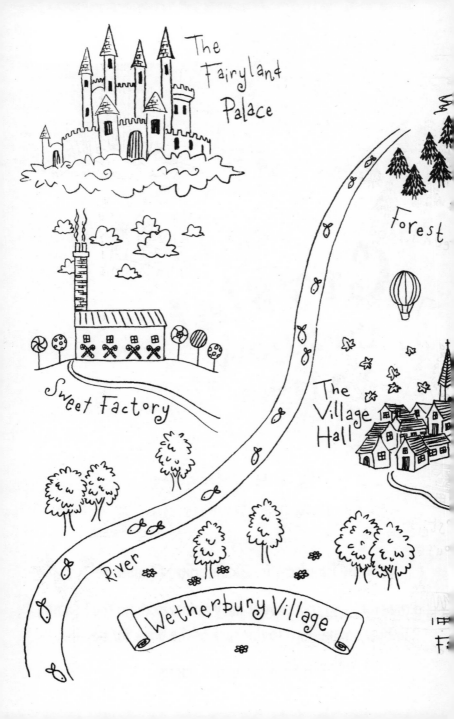

The Weather Fairies

For my friend, Joe Heaney, who has
always been magical to me!

Special thanks to
Narinder Dhami

ORCHARD BOOKS

First published in Great Britain in 2004 by Orchard Books
This edition published in 2016 by The Watts Publishing Group

3 5 7 9 10 8 6 4 2

HiT entertainment

© 2016 Rainbow Magic Limited.
© 2016 HIT Entertainment Limited.
Illustrations © Georgie Ripper 2004

A CIP catalogue record for this book is available from the British Library.

ISBN 978 1 40834 858 1

Printed and bound by CPI Group (UK) Ltd, Croydon, CR0 4YY

MIX
Paper from
responsible sources
FSC® C104740

The paper and board used in this book are made from wood from responsible sources

Orchard Books
An imprint of Hachette Children's Group
Part of The Watts Publishing Group Limited
Carmelite House, 50 Victoria Embankment, London EC4Y 0DZ

An Hachette UK Company
www.hachette.co.uk
www.hachettechildrens.co.uk

Jack Frost's
Ice Castle

een Wood

Mrs. Fordham's Cottage

The Park

Willow Hill

The High St.

The
Museum

sty's
ouse

Fields

Mudhole

rd

N
W—E
S

Goblins green and goblins small,
I cast this spell to make you tall.
As high as the palace you shall grow.
My icy magic makes it so.

Then steal Doodle's magic feathers,
used by the fairies to make all weathers.
Climate chaos I have planned
on Earth, and here, in Fairyland!

Contents

A Magical Surprise

"Isn't it a lovely day, Mum?" Kirsty Tate said happily, as she gazed out of the car window at the blue sky and sunshine. "Do you think it will stay like this all through the summer holidays?"

Mrs Tate laughed. "Well, let's hope so," she said. "Remember what the weather was like on Rainspell

Island? It was always changing!"

Kirsty smiled to herself. She and her parents had been to Rainspell Island on holiday in the last school break. Kirsty had made a new friend, Rachel Walker, there, and the two girls now shared a very special secret. They had helped the seven Rainbow Fairies get back to Fairyland, after Jack Frost had cast a nasty spell to banish them.

"Could Rachel come and stay with us, please, Mum?" Kirsty suggested, as they drew up outside their cottage. The Tates lived in Wetherbury, a pretty village in the middle of the countryside.

"That's a really good idea," Mrs Tate agreed. "Now, let's take the shopping indoors."

"OK," said Kirsty, getting out of the car. "Where's Dad got to?"

"Hello, I'm up here!"

Kirsty glanced up, shading her eyes against the sun. To the left of the house was an old wooden barn. Mr Tate was standing at the top of a ladder, holding a hammer.

"I'm just repairing the roof," he explained. "It's been leaking."

"Oh dear," said Mrs Tate, opening the car boot. She handed two of the shopping bags to Kirsty.

"We must do something about that barn. It's falling down."

"I like it," Kirsty replied. Suddenly she jumped as something cold and wet landed on her nose. "Oh no!" she exclaimed. "I think it's raining." Then she stared at the white flakes which had landed on her pink shirt. "It's not rain," she gasped, "it's snow!"

"Snow?" Mrs Tate looked shocked. "In summer? It can't be!"

But it *was* snowing. In a flash, the sky had turned grey and snowflakes were tumbling down.

"Quick, Kirsty, go indoors!" called Mrs Tate, picking up the rest of the shopping and closing the car boot.

Mr Tate was already climbing down from the ladder. They all rushed inside as the snow swirled around them.

"This is very strange," said Mr Tate, frowning. "I wonder how long it will last?"

Kirsty glanced out of the kitchen window. "Mum, Dad, the snow's stopped!" she cried.

Mr and Mrs Tate joined Kirsty at the window. The sun was shining and the sky was blue. A few puddles of water were all that remained of the sudden snowstorm.

"Well!" said Mr Tate. "How extraordinary! It was almost like magic!"

Kirsty's heart began to thump. Could there be magic in the air? But why should there be? She and Rachel had found the Rainbow Fairies, and Jack Frost had promised not to harm them again. Everything was fine in Fairyland now, wasn't it?

"You'd better go and change out of that wet shirt, Kirsty," said her mum.

Kirsty turned away from the window. As she did so, she spotted something standing on the kitchen table. It was a rusty, old, metal weather-vane in the shape of a cockerel. 'What's that?' she asked.

"I found it in the park this morning," her father said. "It will look great on top of the barn when I've finished fixing the roof."

Kirsty reached out a hand towards the weather-vane. As she did so, the metal glowed, and glittering sparkles danced towards her fingers. Kirsty blinked in surprise. When she looked again, the sparkles had vanished. All she could see was rusty metal once more.

Feeling puzzled, Kirsty ran upstairs to change. Had she imagined the sparkles? The snow was real, though. She was sure of that. "I'll ring Rachel after lunch," she thought. "Maybe she's been noticing strange things, too."

Kirsty hurried into her bedroom. There, on a shelf above her bed, sat the snow dome the fairies had given her. It was a very special thank-you for helping the Rainbow Fairies, and Rachel had one just the same. It was filled with glittering fairy dust, in all the colours of the rainbow. When the snow dome was shaken up, the dust swirled and sparkled.

But right now, no one was shaking the snow dome – and yet the fairy dust was whirling around inside the glass! Kirsty forgot about her wet shirt, and stared at the sparkling snowstorm. She could hardly believe her eyes. "It must be magic!" she told herself.

She dashed across the room and grabbed the glass dome, but with a gasp of pain she dropped it straightaway. The snow dome was so hot it had burnt her fingers!

As the dome fell, it struck the edge of the shelf and shattered.

"Oh, no!" Kirsty exclaimed, dismayed that she'd broken her beautiful gift.

Sparkling fairy dust flew into the air, and floated down around her. But now something else was happening.

Kirsty was shrinking! It was just like before, when she and Rachel had become fairy-sized and visited Fairyland. Now she was tiny all over again.

She twisted round to look over her shoulder. There were her fairy wings, delicate and glittering. "Maybe the fairies want me to fly to Fairyland to see them," Kirsty said to herself. "But I don't know the way."

The sparkling fairy dust was still drifting around her. Suddenly, a strong breeze swept in through the open window. It picked up the fairy dust, whipping it into a whirlwind of glittering sparks. Next moment, the whirlwind lifted Kirsty gently into the air, and carried her out of the window!

Trouble in Fairyland

Kirsty was whisked through the sky in a haze of colourful fairy dust. She flew over rivers, mountains, woods and houses, passing fluffy white clouds on the way. Soon she saw the red and white toadstool houses of Fairyland below her. There was the river, winding its way past the green hills.

The water glittered like diamonds
in the golden sunshine.

The whirlwind was
bringing Kirsty down
now, close to the silver
Fairy Palace with its
pretty pink towers.
Kirsty could see
King Oberon and
Queen Titania
waiting for her
with a group of
fairies. And next
to the Queen was
someone Kirsty
knew very well.

"Rachel!" called Kirsty.

Rachel rushed over, as
Kirsty landed gently on the grass.

22

"I came the same way you did," Rachel explained excitedly, giving Kirsty a hug. "My snow dome broke, and the fairy dust brought me here."

"Do you know why?" asked Kirsty. Rachel shook her head, as the King and Queen and their fairies joined them. "It's wonderful to see you both," beamed Queen Titania. "But I'm afraid we need your help again," she added, looking anxious.

"I hope you don't mind us bringing you here like this?" King Oberon put in.

"Of course not!" Kirsty said eagerly. "What's happened?"

The Queen sighed. "I'm afraid that Jack Frost is up to his old tricks again."

Rachel looked shocked. "But he promised not to harm the Rainbow Fairies anymore!" she said, glancing up at the sky with a shiver. The sun had disappeared and it was suddenly cold.

"Yes," Queen Titania replied. "Unfortunately, he didn't promise not to harm our Weather Fairies!" And she waved her hand at the seven fairies standing around her.

"You mean this strange weather is all because of Jack Frost?" asked Kirsty, as sunshine blazed through the grey clouds once more.

The Queen nodded. "Doodle, our weather-vane cockerel, is in charge of Fairyland's weather," she explained. "Doodle's tail is made up of seven beautiful feathers – each feather controls one kind of weather."

"Every morning, Doodle decides on the best weather for every part of Fairyland," the King went on. "Then he gives each Weather Fairy the correct feather, and off they go to do their weather work."

Rachel and Kirsty were listening hard.

"Come with us," said the Queen. "We'll show you what's happened."

The King and Queen led Rachel and Kirsty into the palace gardens and over to a golden pool. The Queen scattered some fairy dust onto the water, which began to fizz and bubble.

After a moment, it grew still and clear
and a picture began to appear on the
surface. It showed a handsome cockerel
with a magnificent tail of red, gold and
copper coloured feathers.

"That's Doodle," the Queen
explained. "Yesterday morning he
planned the weather for Fairyland, just
as he always does."

Rachel and Kirsty watched as Doodle
flew to the top of the palace and
perched on one of the pink
towers. He spun slowly
round, gazing out over the
hills of Fairyland. Then
he nodded his feathery
head, and flew down again.

"Jack Frost has always helped Doodle
with the wintry weather," the King
continued. "There's so much work, with
all the ice and snow and frost. But now it's
summer, and Jack Frost has nothing to do."

"So he's bored," the Queen put in. "And
that means trouble! Look…" She pointed
at the pictures on top of the water.

Doodle was standing on the palace steps,
waiting for the Weather Fairies to collect
their feathers.

Suddenly Kirsty gasped. "Look, Rachel!" she cried. "The goblins!"

Rachel remembered the goblins. They were Jack Frost's servants, and they were mean and selfish. They had big feet, sharp noses and ugly faces.

Seven goblins were creeping towards Doodle. The cockerel did not see them until it was too late. The goblins reached out and snatched Doodle's tail feathers. Then, grinning and cheering, they ran away.

"Oh no!" said Kirsty, as the cockerel chased after the goblins. "Poor Doodle!"

"It gets worse," the Queen sighed, watching the goblins running and gleefully waving the feathers above their heads. "The goblins escaped into the human world, and Doodle followed them. But without his magic feathers, and away from Fairyland, his strength failed," she explained.

"Doodle has become an ordinary weather-vane," the King said sadly. "We don't even know where he is now."

"We need you to find the goblins," the Queen said. "So that we can get Doodle's tail feathers back. Until then, Doodle is stuck in your world, and our weather is topsy-turvy!" She looked up at the sky as a few raindrops began to fall.

"The goblins are causing weather chaos for humans, too."

"Our Weather Fairies will help you," the King told the girls. "They are Crystal the Snow Fairy, Abigail the Breeze Fairy, Pearl the Cloud Fairy, Goldie the Sunshine Fairy, Evie the Mist Fairy, Storm the Lightning Fairy and Hayley the Rain Fairy."

The fairies gathered round Rachel and Kirsty. "Pleased to meet you!" they cried in silvery voices. "Thank you for helping us!"

"Each Weather Fairy will help you to find her own feather," said the Queen. "And we know the goblins are hiding somewhere here…"

She sprinkled more fairy dust over the water, and the picture changed. Now Rachel and Kirsty could see a pretty village surrounded by lush green fields.

"Oh!" Kirsty exclaimed. "That's Wetherbury! That's where I live. So that's why we had the snowstorm. It was the goblins getting up to mischief."

"What snowstorm?" asked Rachel.

Quickly Kirsty explained. "And I think I know where Doodle is, too," she went on eagerly. "I think he's the rusty old weather-vane my dad found in the park!"

A Snowy Start

"Thank goodness Doodle is safe!" cried the Fairy Queen happily.

"But the snowstorm means that one of the goblins is nearby," the King warned, "with Doodle's magic Snow Feather!"

Kirsty turned to Rachel. "Do you think your parents will let you come and stay with me?" she said. "My mum says it's OK."

"I'll ask them," Rachel replied. "Then we can get the feathers back from the goblins!"

The King nodded. "That's a good idea," he said.

The Queen stepped forward. She had two shining golden lockets in her hand. "Each locket is filled with fairy dust," she explained, giving them to the girls. "You can use a pinch of this to turn yourself into fairies and back to humans again.

But remember!" She smiled at Rachel and Kirsty. "Don't look too hard for magic – it will find you. And when you do see it, you will know that one of the magic feathers is close by."

The girls fastened the lockets around their necks.

"And beware of the goblins," the King added. "Jack Frost has cast a spell to make them bigger."

"Bigger!" Rachel said, feeling nervous. "As big as humans, you mean?"

The King shook his head. "We have
a law in Fairyland that not even
magic can make anything bigger
than the topmost turret of the Fairy
Palace." He pointed at the tallest
pink tower. "But it means that now
the goblins stand almost as high as
your shoulders – when you're
human-sized."

Kirsty shivered. "We'll have to be
careful," she said solemnly. "But of
course we're happy to help."

Rachel nodded.

"Thank you," said the King
gratefully. "We knew you would."

The Queen scattered fairy dust over
the girls. It whipped up around them,
and in a few seconds, a whirlwind was
gently lifting them up into the sky.

"Goodbye!" Kirsty and Rachel called,
waving at their friends below. "And
don't worry. We'll find Doodle's
feathers and bring him safely home."

✿⋆⋅✿⋆

"Rachel's here!" Kirsty shouted, rushing to the front door.

The Walkers' car was just turning into the driveway.

"Put your boots on before you go out in the snow," called Mrs Tate from the kitchen. Kirsty pulled on her boots. It was the day after she and Rachel had been to Fairyland, and Rachel's parents had agreed that Rachel could come and stay with the Tates. Kirsty had been worried that the Walkers wouldn't be able to make it to Wetherbury, though.

The goblins had been up to their tricks
overnight. There had been a heavy
snowfall, and flakes were
still drifting down.

Kirsty dashed outside,
followed by her mum
and dad. The
Walkers were
unloading
Rachel's suitcase
from the car.

"Hello," called
Mr Tate. "Sorry
about the weather.
Isn't it awful?"

"I packed my boots,
scarf and gloves in my
suitcase," Rachel whispered
to Kirsty as they hugged hello.

"Do come in and have a cup of tea," Mrs Tate offered.

"Lovely," Rachel's mum agreed. "But we mustn't stay too long, in case the snow gets worse."

"Come and see Doodle," Kirsty said quietly to Rachel, as their parents chatted.

Mr Tate had put Doodle inside the hall cupboard. Gently, Kirsty lifted the weather-vane out.

"Oh, poor Doodle!" said Rachel when she saw the rusty metal. "We must find his feathers, Kirsty!"

A knock at the front door made them both look round.

"I wonder who that is?" Kirsty said, putting Doodle away again.

Kirsty's mum had opened the door,

and was talking to an elderly lady who was well wrapped up against the cold.

"It's Mum's friend, Mrs Fordham," Kirsty whispered to Rachel. "She lives on Willow Hill."

"I'm sorry to bother you," Mrs Fordham was saying, "but there's so much snow, I can't get back to my cottage. I wondered if I could wait here for a while."

"Of course," said Mrs Tate, helping her inside. "Come and have a cup of tea."

"I've never seen weather like this," Mrs Fordham went on, unwinding her scarf. "And it seems to be worse on Willow Hill than anywhere else. I don't know why."

Kirsty and Rachel glanced at each other.

"Why do you think there's more snow on Willow Hill?" Rachel whispered to Kirsty.

Kirsty looked excited. "Maybe that's where the goblin is with the Snow Feather!"

"Let's go and find out," Rachel suggested.

Kirsty ran to ask her mum if she and Rachel could go out to play in the snow. Meanwhile, Rachel quickly changed out of her summer clothes. They said goodbye to their parents, and hurried outside. It was still snowing.

"Quick," said Kirsty. "We must reach Willow Hill before the goblin gets away."

"Wait for me!" called a silvery voice.

The Grouchy Goblin!

Kirsty and Rachel spun round.

A tiny fairy with crystal-tipped wings was sliding down the drainpipe. She wore a soft blue dress with fluffy white edging. Her wand was tipped with silver. And white scrunchies held her hair in bunches.

"Look! It's Crystal the Snow Fairy!" Kirsty gasped.

The girls rushed over to her.
"Hello again!" Crystal
called. She looked
excited, and tiny,
sparkling snowflakes
fizzed from the
tip of her wand.
"Look at all this
snow," Rachel said.
"We think your
feather is close by."
"So do I," agreed
Crystal. "I can't wait to find it!
But there must be a goblin nearby,
too…" She shivered, and her wings
drooped. "We have to be careful."

"We're going to Willow Hill," Kirsty
explained. "We think the feather may
be over there."

Crystal fluttered down and landed on Rachel's shoulder. "Come on then!" she cried.

They went out of the Tates' garden, and up Twisty Lane into the High Street. There were lots of people around, so Crystal hid herself away in a fold of Rachel's scarf.

Crowds of children were playing in the park, throwing snowballs and building snowmen. They were having fun, but the snow was causing lots of problems, too. The girls passed several cars which were stuck in snowdrifts, and others which had broken down. A burst pipe at the Post Office had flooded the road, and some of the shops were shut.

"How much further is Willow Hill?"
Rachel panted. It was hard work,
tramping through the deep snow.

Kirsty pointed ahead of them. "There
it is," she replied breathlessly.

Rachel's heart sank. The snow-covered
hill looked very high. As they trudged
out of the village, the snow seemed to be
getting deeper, too. It was almost up to
the top of Rachel's boots.

"I've got an idea," Kirsty said suddenly, as her feet sank into a snowdrift. "Why don't we use some of our fairy dust? Then we can fly the rest of the way!" Crystal popped her head out of Rachel's scarf. "Good idea!" she said.

Kirsty and Rachel opened their lockets. They each took a pinch of fairy dust and sprinkled it over themselves. Immediately, they began to shrink, and their wings grew.

"Come on." Crystal took their hands.
"Let's fly to the top of the hill.
I can see a house up there."

"That's Willow Cottage,"
explained Kirsty, "Mrs
Fordham's house."

Crystal and the
girls flew to the
top of the hill,
dodging the falling
snowflakes, which
seemed as big as dinner
plates to Rachel and Kirsty.

As they neared the cottage,
Kirsty spotted smoke coming from
the chimney. "That's funny!" she said,
frowning. "Mrs Fordham lives on her
own, and she's at our house. So who lit
the fire?"

"Let's look inside," suggested Crystal.
They swooped down and hovered
outside a frosty window. Crystal
waved her wand to melt some of the
frost, leaving a small spyhole. They
peered inside.

Sitting on the floor, in front of a
roaring fire, was a big, ugly goblin.

And in his hand was a shimmering copper feather, speckled with a snowy-white colour.

Crystal gasped. "The Snow Feather!" she whispered excitedly.

A Cunning Plan

As Kirsty, Rachel and Crystal watched, the goblin sneezed loudly.

"A-TISH-O-O-O!" A shower of ice cubes clattered on to the floor. They began to melt, leaving little puddles of water here and there.

"The goblin doesn't know how to use the magic feather properly," Crystal whispered.

Kirsty and Rachel felt a bit frightened. The goblin was quite big, because of Jack Frost's spell, and he looked very scary with his ugly face, pointed nose and big, flat feet.

The goblin huddled closer to the fire. He was grumbling, and rubbing his toes. "I'm so cold," he moaned. "And my chilblains hurt!"

Crystal smiled. "Goblins hate to have cold feet!" she murmured.

"How are we going to get the feather back?" asked Kirsty.

"Let's fly round the house and look for a way in," Rachel suggested.

They flew around, checking all the windows and doors. But everything was locked. They could hear the goblin still muttering about his cold feet.

Kirsty grinned. "I've got an idea!" she said. "Dad's just thrown out a pair of slippers that were too small for him. If I wrap them up in a box, I can deliver the parcel to the goblin. Then he'll open the door."

"Perfect!" Crystal agreed, her wand fizzing sparkly snowflakes. "The goblin won't be able to resist a present. And if Rachel and I hide inside the box, maybe we can get the feather back."

Quickly, they flew back to the Tates' house. With a touch of her wand, Crystal turned Kirsty human-sized again. Then she and Rachel hid inside Kirsty's pockets.

Kirsty let herself quietly into the house and found the slippers, which her dad had put in the bin. Then she got an old shoebox, and wrapped the slippers up in lots of tissue paper.

"You can come out now," she whispered to Crystal and Rachel. Luckily, all the parents were chatting to Mrs Fordham in the lounge, and hadn't heard a thing.

Crystal and Rachel flew into the shoebox, and hid under the tissue paper.

Kirsty popped the lid back on the box, and wrapped it neatly in brown paper. Then she set off again for Willow Hill. She couldn't fly up the hill with the parcel, so she had to walk.

By the time she reached Willow Cottage, she was out of breath and wet with snow. "We're here," she said quietly to Crystal and Rachel. Then she knocked on the door, and waited.

There was no reply.
Kirsty lifted the
letter-box. "Delivery!"
she called.

"Go away!" the
goblin shouted crossly.

Kirsty tried again.
"Lovely warm slippers for
Mr Goblin!" she said loudly.

This time the door opened,
just a crack. Kirsty held
the parcel out. The
door opened wider,
and a bony hand
shot out and
grabbed the box.
Then the door
was slammed shut
in Kirsty's face.

Kirsty hurried to the window and peeped in. The goblin was tearing the paper off the shoebox. He pulled out the slippers, popped them on his feet and stomped around the room to try them out. They were a bit big, but he looked delighted. He settled down happily in front of the fire, stretched his toes out to the flames and fell fast asleep. The shining Snow Feather lay on his lap.

Kirsty watched as the tissue paper in the box began to move. Crystal and Rachel fluttered out.

Crystal flew over to the snoring goblin and lifted the feather from his lap.

"You'd better make me human-sized again, Crystal," Rachel whispered. "Then I can open the window and we can escape."

Crystal nodded. She waved her wand over Rachel, who instantly shot up to her full size. Then Rachel unlatched the window and pushed it open.

An icy blast of wind swept into the room.

"What's going on?" the goblin roared, jumping up from his armchair.

A Very Unusual Snowball

"Quick!" Kirsty gasped, pulling Rachel through the window.

Crystal flew out too, her face pale with fear.

The goblin spotted the Snow Fairy and gave another furious roar. He dashed over to the window, jumped out and gave chase.

Kirsty and Rachel hurried down the hill. It was hard to run fast because the snow was so deep.

"Hurry!" Crystal called. She was flying above them, the feather in her hand. "He's getting closer!"

Rachel glanced anxiously over her shoulder. The goblin was catching up!

But then she saw him trip over in his too-big slippers. Yelling loudly, he rolled head over heels down the hill, picking up snow as he went.

"Watch out, Kirsty!" Rachel gasped. "The goblin's become a giant snowball!"

The goblin's arms and legs stuck out of the snowball as it hurtled down the hill. Quickly, the girls flung themselves out of the way. The snowball shot past them, and rolled away, faster and faster. Soon it was out of sight.

"Are you all right?" asked Crystal, flying over to her friends.

They were picking themselves up and brushing snow from their clothes.

"We're fine!" Kirsty beamed. "Can you stop the Snow Feather's magic?"

Crystal nodded and expertly waved the Snow Feather in a complicated pattern. Immediately, the snow clouds vanished. Overhead, the sky was blue and the sun shone. By the time the girls had made their way back to the Tates' cottage, the snow had melted away.

As Kirsty and Rachel entered the house, with Crystal safely hidden in Kirsty's pocket, Mrs Tate smiled.

"Hello, girls," she said. "Isn't it funny how the weather's changed? Your mum and dad have gone home, Rachel. At least they won't have to worry about the snow now."

Kirsty and Rachel grinned at each other.

"Your dad's in the garden, Kirsty," Mrs Tate went on. "He's fixing that old weather-vane to the barn roof."

Kirsty and Rachel dashed outside.

They gazed up at the barn – and
there was Doodle! Mr Tate was busy
in his shed.

"Quick, Crystal." Kirsty took the Snow
Fairy from her pocket. "Give Doodle his
tail feather back!"

Crystal nodded. Fluttering her shiny
wings, she flew up to Doodle, and
slotted the big tail feather into place.

The girls gasped in surprise as copper
and gold sparkles fizzed and flew from
Doodle's tail. The iron weather-vane
vanished. There in its place was Doodle,
as colourful as he had been in Fairyland!

Doodle turned his head, and stared
straight at Kirsty and Rachel. "Beware—"
he squawked. But before he could say
anymore, his feathers began to stiffen
and he became metal again.

"What was he trying to say?" Rachel asked, puzzled.

Kirsty shook her head. She had no idea.

"I don't know either," sighed Crystal. "But it must be important."

"Yes," Crystal agreed. She waved at Rachel and Kirsty. "And now that you've found the Snow Feather, I must return to Fairyland. Goodbye and thank you."

"Goodbye!" Rachel and Kirsty called.

The girls waved as Crystal flew up into the sky, her wings glittering in the sun.

Kirsty turned to Rachel. "And now we only have six magic feathers to find," she said.

Rachel nodded. "I wonder where the next one will be!"

Meet the
Friendship Fairies

When Jack Frost steals the Friendship Fairies' magical objects, BFFs everywhere are in trouble! Can Rachel and Kirsty help save the magic of friendship?

www.rainbowmagicbooks.co.uk

Calling all parents, carers and teachers!
The Rainbow Magic fairies are here to help
your child enter the magical world of reading.
Whatever reading stage they are at, there's
a Rainbow Magic book for everyone!
Here is Lydia the Reading Fairy's guide to
supporting your child's journey at all levels.

Starting Out

Our Rainbow Magic Beginner Readers are perfect for first-time readers who are just beginning to develop reading skills and confidence. Approved by teachers, they contain a full range of educational levelling, as well as lively full-colour illustrations.

Developing Readers

Rainbow Magic Early Readers contain longer stories and wider vocabulary for building stamina and growing confidence. These are adaptations of our most popular Rainbow Magic stories, specially developed for younger readers in conjunction with an Early Years reading consultant, with full-colour illustrations.

Going Solo

The Rainbow Magic chapter books – a mixture of series and one-off specials – contain accessible writing to encourage your child to venture into reading independently. These highly collectible and much-loved magical stories inspire a love of reading to last a lifetime.

www.rainbowmagicbooks.co.uk

"Rainbow Magic got my daughter reading chapter books. Great sparkly covers, cute fairies and traditional stories full of magic that she found impossible to put down" - Mother of Edie (6 years)

"Florence LOVES the Rainbow Magic books. She really enjoys reading now" Mother of Florence (6 years)

Read along the Reading Rainbow!

Well done – you have completed the book!

This book was worth 1 star.

See how far you have climbed on the Reading Rainbow.
The more books you read, the more stars you can colour in
and the closer you will be to becoming a Royal Fairy!

Do you want to print your own Reading Rainbow?

1) Go to the Rainbow Magic website

2) Download and print out the poster

3) Colour in a star for every book you finish
and climb the Reading Rainbow

4) For every step up the rainbow,
you can download your very own certificate

There's all this and lots more at
rainbowmagicbooks.co.uk

You'll find activities, stories, a special newsletter
AND you can search for the fairy with your name!